CLOSE ENCOUNTERS!

SYSTEMS & INTERACTIONS

Written by M. Leontovich

Illustrated by James Cloutier

GoodYearBooks

An Imprint of ScottForesman
A Division of HarperCollinsPublishers

6781579

Acknowledgments
Special thanks to Mark Dow from the Willamette Science and Technology Center (WISTEC) for his insight, corrections, and enthusiasm about science . . . and for knowing (off the top of his head) the weight of a cubic foot of water; to the reference librarians at the Eugene Public Library for their tenacity and good cheer in the face of a sometimes obstructionist computerized card catalogue; to Dick Lennox, Niki Harris, Cornelia Bremer, Steven Mueller, Tamara Kidd, and Percy Franklin for their untiring spirit and hard work in getting this to disk; to Annie Vrijmoet for original design work; to Patrick Fagan for skillful and diplomatic editing on the front lines; and to the scientists, writers, and teachers in my life who explained scientific principles in ways I could understand.

GoodYearBooks
are available for most basic curriculum subjects plus many enrichment areas. For more GoodYearBooks, contact your local bookseller or educational dealer. For a complete catalog with information about other GoodYearBooks, please write:

GoodYearBooks
ScottForesman
1900 East Lake Avenue
Glenview, IL 60025

Illustrated by James Cloutier.
Copyright © 1995 Franklin & Cron Development Group, Inc.
All Rights Reserved.
Printed in the United States of America.

ISBN 0-673-36220-5 (Hardcover)

1 2 3 4 5 6 7 8 9 - DQ - 03 02 01 00 99 98 97 96 95

ISBN 0-673-36215-9 (Softcover)

1 2 3 4 5 6 7 8 9 - DR - 03 02 01 00 99 98 97 96 95

CONTENTS

SAFETY TIPS

1. **Pay attention to all WARNINGS.** They are marked with a label like this:

Good safety practices are necessary for scientists of all ages.

2. **Wear your goggles.** They protect your eyes when mixing household or other chemicals.

3. **Don't be afraid to ask for help from adults.** Lots of adults like doing science experiments, mainly because they haven't had a chance to do any for a long time. Sometimes you may need their help, and sometimes you may want to invite adult family members to join in just for fun!

4. **Treat all substances as potentially hazardous**—for example, as flammable, corrosive, or toxic.

5. **Label all chemicals carefully, use them with adult supervision, and keep them out of the reach of young children.** Most of the chemicals in these investigations are common household substances such as vinegar, salt, and baking soda. Other chemicals are clearly marked with WARNING signs.

6. **Any time you are using the stove or matches, there is danger of fire. Make sure adults are present.**

7. **Be careful when using knives or other sharp instruments.** Wear goggles to protect your eyes.

WHAT CAN YOU DO WHEN AN EXPERIMENT "DOESN'T WORK"?

First of all, don't give up! Consider it a little challenge, and do some problem solving. Think out loud in your journal, asking yourself these questions:

1. What happened? What did you *expect* to happen?
2. Why didn't the experiment work like you thought it would?
3. What surprises did you find? What did you learn from the results?
4. What might you try differently next time? How could you test it out?

Remember: Often the most amazing and important scientific discoveries happen by accident—they are not planned. Mess around. Sometimes science is roll-up-your-sleeves, "thinking-on-your-feet" kind of work.

INTRODUCTION

What do a can of cold soda and a redwood tree have in common?

That question may sound odd, but redwood trees and cold sodas really *do* have something in common (you'll find out what it is in Chapter 1). And did you know your salad dressing can teach you a lot about how sharks swim? or that a pot of spaghetti on your stove may affect rainfall in Paris? or that dogs and cats are good for your health?

As you learn more about how things live and grow, you'll start to see all kinds of connections. Sometimes things eat or breathe in the same way. Sometimes things interact with each other. Sometimes things depend on each other to live. Even though the Earth is a big place, all living things on it have a lot on common. The thing to keep in mind is this: *everything* is connected. Once you know that, then you can start to figure out how.

This book is filled with experiments that show you how things work, or how they interact. After each one, try to think of other connections that aren't talked about in the experiment. Look at the world around you and start asking questions. Does another creature eat (or breathe or behave) in the same way? How does this affect plants? What does this have to do with you? Does it affect where you live, how you dress, or what you eat? Are there any other connections you can find? What would happen if things *didn't* work this way? How would this change the world around you?

Armed with these questions, you're ready to learn a lot about yourself and the world around you. Get ready for some close encounters!

WATER, WATER, EVERYWHERE

Don't look now, but you're surrounded—by water. You probably think you know water when you see it, in lakes, the ocean, or in the bathtub, where it's pretty easy to spot. But water has a few disguises. Right now there is a lot of water in the air around you that you can't see. You're breathing air and water this very minute!

A Brilliant Disguise

Water in the air has a special name: **water vapor.** Water changes to water vapor through **evaporation.** It looks like water is disappearing, but it's really just changing from a liquid to a gas. Sometimes you can see it. The steam over a boiling pot of water is water vapor. Clouds in the sky are water vapor, too. (There will be more about water vapor and clouds in Chapter 4).

And Back Again

Sometimes it all happens backwards, and it looks like water appears out of nowhere. You know those mornings when there is water on the grass even though it didn't rain? Water vapor in the air changed *back* to water again during the night. When water suddenly appears like this, it's called **condensation.**

You see condensation whenever you have a cold drink. The outside of the glass gets dripping wet. It looks like the glass is sweating, but it's not. Water vapor in the air condensed, turning into drops of water all over your glass.

Or have you ever noticed how foggy the mirror is after you take a bath? Water vapor condensed on the mirror.

Have you figured out what makes water change from one disguise to another? The next few experiments should help you become an expert!

A WATERY ENVIRONMENT
There is a lot of water vapor in the air. The average roomful of air contains anywhere from 30 to 50 pounds of water!

Discover more about the energy of water in *Power Up!*, Chapter 7, and its role in the growth of plants in Chapters 3 and 4 of *The Inside Story!*

EXPERIMENT 1: IT'S A GAS

SUPPLIES
2 identical jars
1 sheet of black con-
    struction paper
1 sheet of white paper
magic marker or crayon
tape
water
thermometer (optional)

We know water evaporates. But what makes it evaporate?

1. Find two jars the same size. Pour one cup of water into each one. Make sure the water is at *exactly* the same level. Use your magic marker and draw a line on each jar to show the water level.

2. Tape the black construction paper around the outside of one of the jars. Leave a thin opening down the side so you can see the water level.

Don't cover the top! Now use the white paper and do the same thing to the other jar.

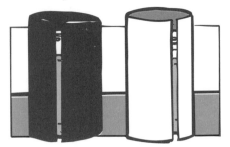

3. Place your jars on a *sunny* window-sill. Check them every day. In your journal, write down the water level. Hold the jars in your hand for a few seconds every day. Which jar is warmer? cooler? If you have a ther-mometer, take the temperature of the water in each jar, and note this in your journal.

After three or four days (or even a week), carefully remove the paper. Make sure you don't spill any water! Look at the original water level lines.

Which jar lost more water, the cooler or the warmer jar? What do you think speeds up evaporation?

THE WET LOOK
You depend on evaporation. Without evaporation, every-thing you washed would stay wet. Imagine going to school with clothes and air that stayed wet all day!

FOOD FOR THOUGHT
What would happen if water *never* turned to water vapor? How would this effect the weather? plants? animals? you?

INVESTIGATE SOME MORE!

Pour 1/2 cup of water into a wide-mouthed jar, 1/2-cup of water into a saucer or shallow bowl, and 1/2-cup of water into a soda bottle. Leave them for a few days. Which one do you think will evaporate the fastest and slowest? Can you guess why?

EXPERIMENT 2: OUT OF THIN AIR

SUPPLIES
small jar, glass, or tin can
water
clear plastic wrap
2 pennies
a rubber band

In the last experiment, you made water disappear. Now you're going to make it appear.

1. Before you start, put one of the pennies in your pocket so it stays warm. Put the other penny in the freezer.

2. Fill your container 1/3 full with warm water. Stretch plastic wrap over the top and hold it in place with a rubber band.

3. Put the warm penny on top of the plastic wrap for a minute.

Now take it off. What happens? Make some notes in your journal. Now take the other penny out of the freezer and place that on the plastic wrap. Leave it there a minute, then take it off. What happens? What do you see on the plastic wrap? What happened to the water vapor in the air in your container, and why? Make some notes in your journal.

4. What do you think makes water vapor condense and turn to water droplets? How does the penny experiment explain condensation?

WHAT A DRIP
Condensation helps the giant redwood trees of California when they're thirsty. Redwoods grow when there's lots of fog. The fog condenses on their leaves and drips down to the earth, providing lots of water for their thirsty roots.

INVESTIGATE SOME MORE!
List and draw some examples of condensation in your science journal. What do they all have in common? In each case, what is the water and air temperature? What surfaces does water condense on?

11/12 CONDENSATION
① Water was on the grass this morning. The air was pretty cool.
③ My glasses fogged up when I went into school this morning. The air in school was warm, but it was chilly outside.

EXPLORE SOME MORE

CLUES IN THE CLOUDS

Do you think all clouds look alike? Think again! Clouds have many different shapes. Scientists have given these shapes different names. Check outside the window and see if you can spot any of the clouds shown in the illustrations below. Draw and describe in your journal any others you see. Then write down what the weather is like that day. Do this every day for a week or two. Can cloud shapes help you *predict* the weather? Make some predictions in your journal. Maybe you can get a job as a weather forecaster!

Cirrus clouds look like thin wisps of hair that curl up at the end (the word "cirrus" means "curl of hair" in Latin).

Cumulus is a Latin word meaning "heap." That's what cumulus clouds look like—a heap of clouds (or a heap of mashed potatoes!).

Did you ever draw a picture of a sky with a few fluffy clouds in it? You were drawing cumulus clouds.

A **cumulonimbus** cloud is the giant of clouds. Cloud is heaped upon cloud, sometimes up to eleven miles high!

Stratus means "layer." When the whole sky looks like a blanket of gray, you're looking at stratus clouds.

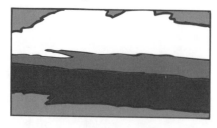

LIVING IN THE CLOUDS

Wouldn't it be fun to live in the clouds? You can do the next best thing and bring the clouds down to your room. All you need is some paint, paper, and a few "cloud makers."

Before you start, decide where and what you're going to paint. Maybe it can be a family project to repaint part of your room—perhaps just one wall or the ceiling. If painting a wall is out of the question, use large sheets of butcher paper you can hang up later.

Start by painting your sky. Use lots of blues, or make a sunset by adding some red and orange. When the paint is dry, it's time to use your special "cloud makers"—sponges! Fat round sponges work the best. Some stores sell sea sponges—they work great! Dip your sponge into white paint and dab big round shapes on your sky. Try different amounts of paint on your sponge for different effects. Sometimes just a little paint gives a nice fluffy look. Now you can tell everyone you're sleeping in the clouds!

FORESTS IN THE CLOUDS

In the Andes, some rainforests are so high they are nearly always in the clouds. These cool weather rainforests are called *cloud forests*.

I HAVE SOME FRIENDS LIKE THAT... ALWAYS WALKING AROUND WITH THEIR HEADS IN THE CLOUDS

ANDEAN RAINFOREST

FOR FURTHER EXPLORATION
The Weather Sky by Bruce McMillan (New York: Farrar, Straus, Giroux, 1991).
The Science Book of Water by Neil Ardley (New York: Harcourt, Brace, Jovanovich, 1991).

CHAPTER 2

NO SWEAT!

What's the first thing that happens when you say "I don't feel good"? You're right, someone runs for the thermometer and takes your temperature.

Your body likes to keep close to the same temperature all the time, but this is not always easy for your body to do. When it's very hot out, or when you get a lot of exercise, for instance, your body heats up. What does your body do when it gets really hot?

Sweat! Whenever it's very hot out, or you exercise, your body starts sweating. Your skin has little holes called **pores**, and sweat comes out through these pores to the surface of your skin. This is why you get thirsty on hot days. Your body loses lots of water through sweating, and it wants to replace that lost water.

A Mysterious Disappearance

Just imagine all that sweat on your skin. Is it still there an hour later? No—it disappeared. It *evaporates*, just like the water in our last chapter. Why does your body bother making all this sweat if it's just going to evaporate? How does it help to keep your body the right temperature?

In your science journal, make a list of things you do to cool off when you're hot.

Is there anything they all have in common? How do they help cool you down? Use this list to figure out why sweating might be a good idea. Then try Experiment 1, and see if that gives you any more clues.

HOT DOG

Dogs don't sweat to stay cool. (It would all get stuck on their fur, anyway.) Watch a dog on a hot day, or after running. They cool off by panting. Their tongues and lungs get rid of heat this way. If your dog pants for a long time, he or she may be *too* hot. Find a cool, shady place and offer your dog a bowl of water.

FOOD FOR THOUGHT

Why is staying the same temperature so important, anyway? Why can't our body temperature go from 50 degrees to 140 degrees? Investigate other animals for clues, especially reptiles and mammals that hibernate. What happens to other animals when their body temperature gets very low, or very high?

EXPERIMENT 1: HOT STUFF

SUPPLIES
2 thermometers
2 cotton balls
water
rubbing alcohol
a friend

1. Put two thermometers side by side on a table. Dip a cotton ball into water and dab the bottom of one of the thermometers (the red bulb on the bottom) to get it wet. Blow on the wet part to help the water evaporate. What happens?

2. Line up your thermometers again. Make sure they both say the same temperature. Dab the bottom of one with water, and the bottom of the other with alcohol. Blow on the wet parts. Check the temperature of each. Keep track of which one gets dry first. What happened? Can you guess why?

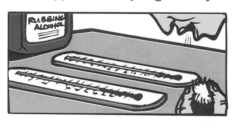

3. Now try it on a friend. Put a dab of water on one arm, and a dab of alcohol on the other (don't tell them which is which).

Which one evaporated the fastest? Which one feels cooler? What does this tell you about the effect of evaporation? Now that you've tried this experiment, why do you think the body makes sweat when you're hot? Why is evaporation important to people?

WARM FUZZIES

Your skin keeps you warm, too. When you're cold, the hair on your skin stands straight up. The hair traps a layer of warmer air near your body. You're fluffing up your "fur," just like animals do when it's cold.

INVESTIGATE SOME MORE!

What if we couldn't sweat? In your science journal, design a human body that cools off some other way. How could we keep cool without sweating? Would we look different? Would we dress differently? Include illustrations of your ideas in your journal.

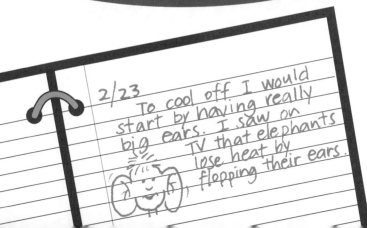

2/23 To cool off I would start by having really big ears. I saw on TV that elephants lose heat by flopping their ears.

EXPERIMENT 2: BE PREPARED

SUPPLIES
water
measuring cup
cornstarch
iodine (you can buy
   iodine at a drugstore)
white paper
bowl
sissors

Your body is always prepared. It has lots of sweat glands to make sweat, just in case you get hot. They're very small, but in this experiment you'll find some and see where they are.

1. Mix together 1/2 cup of water and two tablespoons of cornstarch in a bowl.

2. Cut a piece of paper about the size of the palm of your hand. Dip the white paper into the bowl until it's coated with the cornstarch mixture. Leave the paper out to dry.

3. *Have an adult* paint the palms of your hands with iodine, and then run around and exercise.

WARNING IODINE IS POISONOUS! DO NOT DRINK IT! ONLY APPLY IT TO YOUR SKIN, AND USE AS LITTLE AS POSSIBLE.

When you start sweating, you're ready for the next part.

4. Take the paper and hold it against one of your palms.

See the black dots on the paper? That's where your sweat comes out onto the surface of your skin. When iodine gets wet from the sweat, it turns the cornstarch black.

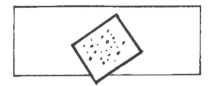

NO SWEAT?
You usually give off two pints (4 cups) a day of sweat. If it's very hot, you'll sweat 4 pints (8 cups) an *hour!* What do you think is most important to do when it's extremely hot outside, or your body is working very hard?

BE COOL, DUDE ... DRINK LOTS OF FLUIDS!!

INVESTIGATE SOME MORE!

Exercise until you start to sweat. Where on your body are you sweating the most? the least? Write your findings in your science journal. Why do you think you sweat more in some places than in others? Are there places where you don't sweat at all? Why?

EXPLORE SOME MORE

COOL CLOTHES

Another way you keep your body the right temperature is by changing your clothes.

Try on different kinds of clothing and walk around in them for a minute. Try to stand outside in the sun if you can. Which ones are good for hot weather? cold weather? sunny weather? dry weather? wet weather?

Try on the clothes made from these materials (the labels inside the clothes should tell you what they're made of):

cotton	wool	silk
leather	fur	polyester
nylon	acrylic	cotton and polyester blend

Try on different colors, especially black and white.

Try different lengths, including something:

long	short
loose	tight

How did these different clothes make you feel? Which ones made you feel cool? warm? sweaty? What effect did color have? Write down the effects of each type of material in your science

journal. Are there any clothes you wear that aren't "practical" choices?

Now imagine you're taking a trip from the Amazon jungle to the Arctic Circle. Design your own clothes for the journey, choosing the materials, colors, and lengths of clothing to keep your body at the right temperature. Draw your creations in your journal.

MAKE YOUR OWN ADOBE

In the southwest United States, many people live in the high desert. The weather there is very sunny, with hot days and cool nights. For centuries, people there have been making bricks out of mud they dry in the sun. They call this material **adobe** (ah DOE bee). They use adobe bricks to make houses. You can make your own small adobe bricks and build a miniature adobe house. You will need some dirt, straw, sand, and water, along with a mixing bowl, mixing spoon, and ice cube tray.

1. Mix 2 cups of dirt with water in a large mixing bowl. Add just enough water to make a thick mud (the amount of water changes depending on the dirt).

2. Add bits of straw and sand a little at a time until the mud gets very hard to mix.

3. Scoop the mud into the ice cube tray. Keep it someplace warm and sunny for two weeks (a sunny windowsill is a good place).

4. After two weeks, take one of the adobe cubes out of the tray and drop it on the floor or outside on the cement. Really! If it breaks, it's not ready yet. Leave it on the windowsill for a few more days. Then drop another one. When you drop a brick and it doesn't break, your adobe is ready.

THIS IS THE PART I LIKE LEAST ABOUT BEING A BRICK!

5. Use your adobe bricks to build a model house. But remember to keep them dry. Adobe will turn to mud again if it gets wet.

Try leaving your adobe on a sunny windowsill during the day. At night, touch the adobe. Is it warm or cool? Why might this be a good house for the high desert, where it's warm during the day and cool at night?

FOR FURTHER EXPLORATION
The Human Body by Bartel Bruun & Ruth Dowling Bruun (New York: Random House, 1982).

STRIVE TO SURVIVE

People aren't the only ones who need water to survive. Plants need water, too. Have you ever forgotten to water one? What happened?

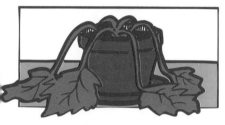

And even when you give plants water, in a week or two (or three) they need more. Where does all that water go?

It turns out that plants also lose water through evaporation. They don't sweat like we do, but they do have pores in their leaves called **stomata.** Water evaporates from the pores. When plants lose water this way, it's called **transpiration.**

When plants get thirsty, they can't go to the fridge and get a drink.

If they live where it rains a lot, they can wait for a good rainshower. But what if they live where it almost never rains, such as in a desert? How can a plant hold onto water so it doesn't wilt and die?

Maybe you've noticed that all plants don't look alike. That's one way plants survive—by having just the right kind of leaves, roots, and flowers for where they live. This is called **adaptation.** All

living things adapt in all kinds of ways: Animals that live in cold places may adapt by having thick fur, for example, or by hibernating all winter. Desert plants have adapted in special ways to live in the desert.

Think of ways a plant might adapt to living in a place where it doesn't rain very often. What kind of plant would do well in a desert? What kind of leaves would it have? What kind of roots? Draw some designs in your journal. The next experiment will help you with your ideas.

BIG THIRST
The saguaro cactus lives in the deserts of the southwest United States. It can survive even if it doesn't rain for several years. When it does rain, it can drink up to half a ton of water after one rain-storm!

Find out more about how the structure of plants enables them to survive in different environments in *The Inside Story!*, Chapters 3 and 4.

EXPERIMENT 1: SPINES BY DESIGN

How can different shaped leaves help a plant save or lose water?

1. Wet 3 paper towels just until they're damp. Not too wet! Pretend they're leaves.

2. Place one sheet on a windowsill in the sun. Imagine that this sheet is like a wide, flat plant leaf.

3. Roll up the second damp sheet.

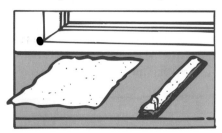

Once it's rolled up, put it on the windowsill next to the other one. This "leaf" is a little different—it's plump instead of flat.

4. Roll up the third damp sheet, and roll a sheet of waxed paper over it. Fold over the ends of the waxed paper so none of the paper towel shows. Tape down the ends.

Put this sheet next to the other two on the windowsill. This leaf resembles the spines on a cactus, which are covered with a waxy coating.

5. Leave all 3 paper towels on the windowsill until the next day. In the meantime, write some notes in your journal. What do you think will happen? Which leaf do you think will hold the most water and why?

6. Check the leaves the next day. Unroll the two that are rolled up. Are any of them still damp? Was your guess right? Which held the most water? Which leaf would be best in a rainforest? a desert? your backyard?

DON'T LOOK NOW
Leaves adapt in all kinds of ways. Some plants have sticky leaves to trap insects. Once the insect is trapped, the plant eats it for lunch.

FLY-IN CAFE

I HEARD THIS NEW PLACE HAS GREAT FOOD BUT LOUSY SERVICE!

FOOD FOR THOUGHT
You can see that plants adapt to different places. So do animals. Look at yourself in the mirror: What is the human body adapted to do? In what kind of climate is our body designed to live? What other animals have arms that can swing in circles like we do? How are we different from other animals? How are we the same? What's the point of having such big brains?

INVESTIGATE SOME MORE!
Go leaf hunting. Draw different leaves in your science journal. Write down what they look like. Are they thin? fat? waxy? juicy? Which leaves do you think lose the most water? Why? Can you make guesses about how rainy or sunny a place is just by looking at the leaves of plants?

SUPPLIES
large glass terrarium
(fishbowls or aquari-
ums are great) or
planter
small cactus plant
small fern
sand
water

EXPERIMENT 2: MADE FOR EACH OTHER

Can a plant that's adapted to one place live in another place? In this experiment, you'll grow two different plants side by side. One plant will be a fern. One will be a cactus. Will they both like living in the same place? We'll see.

1. Put several inches of sand in the terrarium or planter. This will be a desert terrarium, and deserts have very sandy soil. Carefully dig holes for the roots of the two plants. Turn over the pot the fern is in and tap gently until it falls out. Plant it in one of the holes *right away!* (Plants don't like their roots in the air.) Do the same thing with the cactus. Give them each a little water.

2. Place the terrarium where it will get lots of sun every day.

To grow your own ferns, see *On the Move!*, Chapter 7.

3. Give your plants a little water every *month*.

4. In your science journal, draw pictures of your plants the first day. Keep notes on how the plants look. Check them every two days and draw what you see. What changes are happening in your terrarium? What do you think the weather is like where the cactus usually lives? What do you think the weather is like where ferns like to live? How can adaptation help a plant? hurt a plant?

5. Which of the two plants had to adapt? Did it? How?

NOT TO MENTION THE FABULOUS VIEW
Some plants don't have to worry about their soil—they grow on trees! "Air plants" like orchids grow on trees and get their water by absorbing it from the air, or by having leaves shaped like cups which catch and hold rain.

INVESTIGATE SOME MORE!

In your science journal, draw as many kinds of roots as you can think of. Pull up some weeds in your neighborhood or yard and look at the roots (be sure to ask permission first!). What kind of roots would be good for living in dry places? rainy places? rocky soil? rich soil? swampy soil? List your reasons for each guess.

5/28 ROOTS
Dandelion- really long, long skinny root.

Clover-had lots of small, short roots.

Grass- this kind had roots that spread out underground.

EXPLORE SOME MORE

MMM, GOOD... CACTUS TACOS!

Now that you know so much about cactus plants, it's high time you ate one! This recipe makes taco filling using chicken and *nopales*, a kind of cactus. You can buy *nopales* in cans in the Mexican food section of most supermarkets. People who live in deserts have been eating cactus for thousands of years. If you've never eaten cactus, it's time to try some!

WARNING HOT STOVES CAN BE DANGEROUS! HAVE AN ADULT HELP YOU.

3 tablespoons butter
2 cloves garlic minced or crushed
1/2 chopped onion
2 cups shredded chicken (or beef)
2 cans chopped chipotle chiles (or anaheim chiles)
1 cup tomatoes, fresh or canned, chopped
2 cups chopped nopales
taco shells
skillet
mixing spoon

1. In a skillet, melt the butter. Add the chopped onion and garlic. Cook until you can see through the onions.

2. Add everything else to the pan. Cook everything together over low heat for 15 minutes.

3. Fill your taco shell. Feel free to add anything else you like in your tacos: shredded lettuce, cheese, salsa, sour cream, refried beans—the works!

A PLANT HUNT

Botany is the study of plants. The places where all kinds of plants are studied and grown are called **botanical gardens** or **arboretums** (they're like zoos for plants). There may be a botanical garden near where you live. Visit a botanical garden and take the checklist below. How many plants can you find to match the descriptions below? Make some guesses about why each plant adapted in that way.

____ a plant that eats insects

DROP IN FOR LUNCH GUYS.. NO RESERVATIONS NEEDED!

____ a plant that only blooms at night

____ a plant that bats like to visit

____ a plant that is good to eat

____ a plant that is poisonous

____ a plant people use to make medicine

____ a plant that smells really, really bad

____ a plant that is endangered (it might become extinct)

____ a plant that depends on animals to spread its seeds

____ a plant that loses its leaves each year

Ask a botanist who works there for information, including any interesting facts about strange plants. Why did they decide to study plants? Did they like plants when they were kids?

FORGET MIGHTY MUTANT RANGERS! I WANT A BRODIAEA LAXA, AN OXALIS OREGANA, AND A ROSA RUBIGINOSA.

FOR FURTHER EXPLORATION

Life in the Deserts by Lucy Baker (New York: Franklin Watts, 1990).

Secrets of Animal Survival (Washington, DC: National Geographic Society, 1983).

Houses of . . . by Bonnie Shemie (Plattsburgh, NY: Tundra Books, 1991). (A series of books about homes built by Native Americans.)

CREATE A LANDSCAPE

How come we never run out of rain? Think of all the times you've seen it rain in your life. Too many times to count, probably. Where did all that rain come from? Will all the rain ever be used up?

Think back to a rainy day. There are lots of puddles on the sidewalk. In a day or so, the sidewalk is dry again. The water all evaporated! It turned into water vapor and rose into the air.

Since you're becoming an expert on evaporation, you know what water vapor is. You also know that water vapor is *warm*. Warm air (and water vapor) rises. It keeps rising until it gets way up in the sky, forming clouds.

It's cold up there. When the water vapor gets too cool, it turns into water (remember Chapter 1?). That's exactly what happens with clouds, too. When they get too cold, the water vapor condenses and comes down as rain (or snow or hail). This is called the **water cycle:** *Water evaporates, rises into clouds, condenses, and rains down on us. Then it starts evaporating again.*

So, no matter how much it rains, we'll never run out. Just think: The water boiling on your stove today may be raining on the ocean in three weeks. The hailstone that hit your nose last week may have been in an Amazon waterfall last month!

All this rain does more than just water plants. Did you know rain changes the view outside your window? In your science journal, draw pictures of how your neighborhood would look if it rained a lot more. Then draw a picture showing how your neighborhood would look if it rained less. Would the plants be different? What about the houses? Would there be a lake in your living room or a desert outside your door?

RECYCLING, INDEED!
The same water has been falling , evaporating, and falling again for millions of years. Part of the water in that raindrop that hit you may once have hit a tyrannosaurus!

For more experiments on the water cycle see *On the Move!*, Chapter 6.

EXPERIMENT 1: THE WORLD IN A BOX

Time to create the whole world—in a box! Even though you know the Earth isn't flat, it will still show the water cycle in action.

1. Line your box with plastic wrap or a plastic garbage bag. (It may get wet on your world, and the box will fall apart if it gets soggy.) Fill the box with two or three inches of soil.

2. Make a hole in the soil for the bowl or saucer. Place the bowl so the edge is level with the soil. Fill the bowl with water.

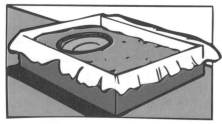

This is your ocean. The Earth is mostly covered with water, so you might want to use two bowls. Just make sure there's more ocean than land, just like on the Earth.

3. Cover the whole box with clear plastic. This is the edge of the sky on your Earth. Put the box on a sunny windowsill. (The Earth gets lots of sunshine).

4. Check your Earth every day. In your science journal, write down what you see. Is the soil wet or dry? Has it been raining on your Earth? Do you think your Earth will run out of rain? Is the landscape different than when you started?

BRING AN UMBRELLA
It rains or snows everywhere, but some places get more rain than others. Mount Waialeah in Hawaii is the rainiest place on Earth, averaging 460 inches (38 feet) of rain a year!

TRUST ME.. IT WON'T BE BIG ENOUGH!

INVESTIGATE SOME MORE!
Add some small plant seeds to your box (there are lots of plants on Earth). Is this a good place for your plants to grow?

5/17
DAY 1:
Today I put the box together and so nothing is really happening yet.

DAY 2:
Things are different today... First I checked the soil to see what changes had taken place.

EXPERIMENT 2: THE SALT FLATS

SUPPLIES
water
large shallow box
soil
sand
salt or baking soda
plastic sheets or a
   garbage bag
large mixing bowl

You've probably seen the salt flats of Utah on TV. They're white and flat and go on for miles. Since they're so flat, people test race cars and rocket cars on them. The cars can go a long time without running into anything. Lots of other places have salt flats, too, but these are probably the most famous.

The flats in Utah were once part of the Great Salt Lake. Water kept evaporating from the lake, and the lake shrank. Salt was left behind as the water evaporated, making the dry salt flats. You can make your own salt flats. Think of it as a Great Salt Lake in a box.

1. Line your box with the plastic sheets or garbage bag. Fill the box with a mixture of half soil and half sand (it's sandy at the salt flats). Press it down in the box. Make the soil in one part lower than the rest. This will be your lake.

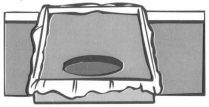

2. Fill a large bowl full of water. Add two or three cups of baking soda or salt so it's very salty. Stir until the salt dissolves.

3. Fill your box with the solution of water and salt. Make sure *all* the soil is covered with a thin layer of water.

You may need to add more water and salt to do this. When you can't see any more soil, you have enough.

4. Put the box on a sunny windowsill. (It's sunny in Utah.) Don't cover it!

5. Watch your salt flats every day. What happens? What would happen if it rained a lot there? What do you think would happen to the Great Salt Lake in Utah?

WHAT STOP SIGN?
Many of the cars that race on the salt flats have broken records for speed. Some of the cars go over 600 miles an hour!

MOONSCAPES
Think about the landscape on the moon. Look in books for pictures of the moon. Why is it so different from Earth? What would you have to do to make it more like Earth? Could it be done?

How does water change the landscape? See *On the Move!*, Chapter 2, Experiment 1.

INVESTIGATE SOME MORE!
Do the experiment over again, this time covering the box with a sheet of clear plastic so it "rains" a lot. What happens this time? How does rain change the landscape?

EXPLORE SOME MORE

THINK IT'LL RAIN?

If you ever watch the weather report, you know it's hard to predict the weather. But there are ways to make good guesses. You can start by making your own barometer.

Barometers measure **air pressure.** Air pressure is the air pressing down on the earth. If the air isn't pressing down too much, it's called low pressure. That usually means wet weather—but not always! That's why it's so hard to predict the weather! If it presses harder, it's called high pressure. That means a nice day—well, usually! (You can see why weather forecasters have a tough job).

Once you make a barometer at home you can keep track of high and low pressure, and see if that means good or bad weather where you live. You'll need:

glass jar with a wide mouth (a canning jar or mayonnaise jar is good)
balloon
straw
stiff paper or cardboard
rubber band
tape

1. Stretch the balloon tightly over the mouth of the jar. You may want to cut the balloon open first to make it easier. Make sure you stretch the balloon as

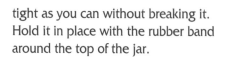

tight as you can without breaking it. Hold it in place with the rubber band around the top of the jar.

2. Cut the straw at an angle so it has a point at one end. Tape the other end of the straw *flat* on top of the stretched balloon. The straw should be straight across the top, not tilted up or down.

3. Find a place to keep your barometer (a desk, for example.) Tape the paper against the wall there. Position the jar so the pointy end of the straw just barely touches the cardboard. Make a mark on the paper where it touches.

4. Over the next week or two, keep checking to see where the straw touches the cardboard. Make a mark there. As the air pressure changes, it will press down on the balloon, changing the position of the straw slightly.

After a few weeks, you'll see there are high marks and low marks. These tell you if there is high or low air pressure today. They will also help you tell when it is changing, going up or down. This tells you the weather will be changing, too.

5. In your science journal, make a chart. Write down whether the air pressure that day is high or low. Then write down whether it is rising or falling. Looking at your chart, make some predictions about the weather. Is it getting nicer? Will it get stormy soon? Keep track of your predictions. Were you right?

Make another page in your science journal next to your page on air pressure. Label this one CLOUDS. Every day, go out and look at the shapes of clouds. Are they cirrus? stratus? cumulus? Put this down next to your air pressure readings. Do these help you predict the weather better?

LOOKS LIKE JETTOSTRATUS TO ME...!

FOR FURTHER EXPLORATION
The Sierra Club Book of Weatherwisdom by Vicki McVey (Boston: Little, Brown, 1991).
Eyewitness Books: Weather by Brian Cosgrove (New York: Knopf, 1991).

THE GREAT MOLECULE MIGRATION

Everything you see is made up of tiny particles called molecules. This includes you, the earth, water, this book, the air, your chair—everything! These tiny molecules are moving all the time. Molecules in gases, like air, are very far apart, so they move around a lot. Molecules in solids, like this book, are very close together and don't move very much at all (if they did, it would be very hard to read!).

If Molecules Threw a Party

To get an idea of how gas molecules move, imagine a big room, like the gym at school. Now imagine the gym is full of boys, covering the whole gym, except for one corner. That corner is full of girls only. This is how a party of two kinds of molecules would start out. But, remember, molecules move! So, now imagine all the girls slowly spreading out until they're all over the room.

This is what molecules do too. They move from places where there are lots of molecules like themselves (like the girls in the corner) to places where there are not so many molecules like themselves (the rest of the room). In other words, molecules migrate. The scientific term for this migration is **diffusion.**

If you can't see molecules moving, how can you prove they do? Get ready to watch (and smell!) the great molecule migration.

WHOA!

There are 5 billion people on Earth. Water molecules are so small, there are 33 *billion billion* of them in just one drop of water!

DIFFUSION ALERT!

Beware of diffusion in your refrigerator! Wrap up smelly foods or their smell will diffuse into all the other stuff in your refrigerator. Unless, of course, you like it when your chocolate pudding tasts like fried fish.

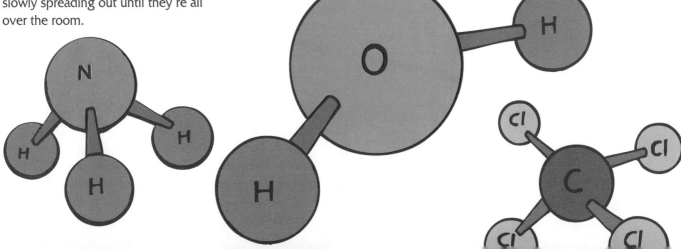

EXPERIMENT 1: THE GLASS IS ALWAYS GREENER

SUPPLIES
2 glasses
salt
food dye
water
measuring cup
measuring spoons

Can you mix things without ever touching them? Can diffusion do all the work for you? In this experiment you will put two liquids close together and find out.

1. Fill the glass with 1/2 cup of water.

2. Add a teaspoon of salt to the water and stir until you can't see any salt crystals.

3. Add drops of food coloring to make the water a beautiful dark color.

4. Fill the second glass with 1/2 cup of water.

5. Slowly pour the colored water into the glass of clear water. Tilt the glass and pour the colored water against the *side* of the other glass, so the two liquids mix as little as possible.

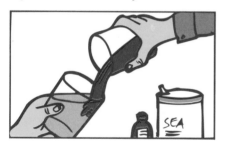

Now put the glass somewhere out of the way, and DON'T TOUCH OR MOVE THE GLASS AGAIN. (We don't want to mix the liquids by moving the glass too much. That would be cheating.)

6. Watch the glass for a few minutes. Take out your science journal and draw a picture of what you see. Come back again in two hours or so and draw another picture. Keep checking on the glass, taking notes or drawing pictures of what you see. What happens? Do you think the molecules are moving? Do you think you can mix something without ever touching it?

INVESTIGATE SOME MORE!

Make another solution of salty, colored water. Pour this *directly* into the glass of tap water. What do you think the effect of adding salt will be? Is your prediction correct? What happens if you make an extra-salty solution? a less salty one?

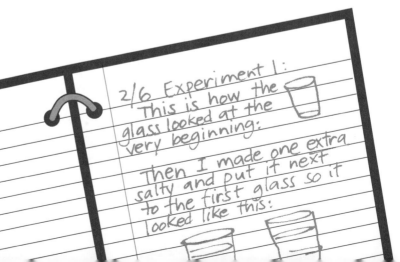

2/6 Experiment 1:
This is how the glass looked at the very beginning:

Then I made one extra salty and put it next to the first glass so it looked like this:

balloon
perfume (or you can use
    vanilla or almond
    extract)
eyedropper
box with a lid or a top
your nose

EXPERIMENT 2: THE NOSE KNOWS

We said that molecules are very tiny, so tiny, in fact, that you can't see one. They're so tiny you can't feel one. So how can you tell if they move from one place to another? Don't worry, there's one part of your body that can find them easily—your nose!

THE FAMOUS NOSE BROTHERS POSSE LEADING THE GREAT MOLECULE CHASE ACROSS TEXAS IN 1878

1. Use your eyedropper to place 10 drops of perfume (or vanilla extract) in the balloon.

PERFUME

2. Hold the bottom of the balloon toward the floor so the perfume doesn't run out. (It tastes really bad!) and blow up the balloon.

Knot the balloon tightly—you don't want air (or perfume) to escape!

3. Put the balloon in a small box. Put the lid on the box and place it in a closet for an hour or two.

4. When the time is up, open the box and take a big whiff. What happened?

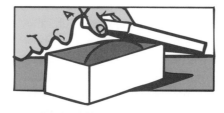

SUPERIOR SNIFFERS
Scientists have proven that girls have a better sense of smell than boys. No one knows why they do. Any ideas?

MAYBE IT'S NATURE'S WAY OF HELPING US TO SMELL SOMETHING FISHY WHEN SOMEONE EXAGGERATES......!!

YOU'RE SO NOSY!
Why do we need a sense of smell or taste? Why do our nose and mouth bother finding molecules and telling us what they are? What would happen if they didn't? How do these senses help us survive? Do other creatures need them more than we do? Why?

INVESTIGATE SOME MORE!
Take a deep sniff. What do you smell? Where's the smell coming from? Write a story in your science journal titled "The Journey of a Molecule." This true-life adventure can tell the story of where the molecule started and how it got all the way to your nose.

EXPLORE SOME MORE

DO YOU HAVE A GOURMET NOSE?

Your nose is finding migrating molecules all the time. Did you ever walk in the door and smell dinner cooking? The molecules from the food in the kitchen have migrated all the way over to the front door.

Investigate smell and taste with your friends. Supplies required for this investigation are: blindfold, 1/2 onion, peeled, 1/2 apple, peeled, and a friend.

1. Put the blindfold on your friend. Then have them hold their nose so they can't smell anything.

2. Tell them you are going to give them some food to try and will then ask them how it tastes. (Let your friend know it's nothing bad.) *Don't tell them what it is!* First, give them a bite of the peeled onion to taste. Then give them a bite of the apple.

3. Ask them how each one tasted. Did holding their nose make any difference in how the foods tasted?

4. Try the experiment again, only this time, wave a piece of onion under your friend's nose while they eat a piece of apple. What do you think the apple tastes like? What have you learned about your sense of taste?

HEY, THIS ROOM SMELLS GOOD!

Everybody likes things that smell good. That's why stores sell so many kinds of sprays to make your house smell nice. Lots of people make their own air freshener. They mix together dried flowers and perfumes and leave them in bowls around the room. The name for this is **potpourri** (poh purr EE).

Here's a recipe for making your own potpourri. Keep it in bowls around the house, or give it as a gift. You can buy most of the ingredients at a natural foods store. They sell dried flowers and oils out of big jars or bins. You can take out and buy just the amount you need. There is usually a scale next to all the dried flowers that measures weight in ounces. In the recipe below, "oz." is short for ounce.

  2 oz. rose petals
  1 oz. lavender
  1/2 oz. lemon verbena
  2 tablespoons crushed orange peel
  1/2 tablespoon crushed cloves
  2 tablespoons powdered orris root
  3 drops rose oil
  2 drops lavender oil
  plastic bag
  bowl
  mixing spoon

In a large bowl, mix together everything except the oils. Add the drops of oil last, one drop at a time. Mix after each drop. When all the oil is added, put the potpourri in a plastic bag for three weeks, so the smells blend together. Shake the bag every day to help blend the smells. After three weeks, place the potpourri in bowls around the house, or wrap it and give it to someone special as a gift.

Make a dream pillow with your potpourri! See *Power Up!*, Chapter 6.

FOR FURTHER EXPLORATION
Eyewitness Books: Matter by
  Christopher Cooper (New York:
  Dorling Kindersley, 1992).
Solids Liquids and Gases by
  Jacqueline Barber (Berkeley, CA:
  Lawrence Hall of Science, 1986).

DIFFUSE YOUR DINNER

All living things are made of tiny cells. Plants have cells, people have cells, animals have cells. You've probably heard of some of them: blood cells, brain cells, or fat cells, for example. Each cell has its own special job to do in our body. To do the job, it needs energy. That's why we eat—to get energy so all the cells in our body can do their work.

Just One Problem

Cells need to eat, just like we do. But they don't have mouths! In fact, they're covered all over with a thin wall called a **cell membrane.** It keeps the insides of the cell from spilling all over the place. To get an idea of what a cell looks like, imagine a balloon filled with jello. The jello is the inside of the cell. The balloon is the cell membrane. The balloon holds it all together. But still, how can cells get the food they need with a wall in the way?

Migrating Molecules to the Rescue!

Lucky for us, molecules like to move! And molecules are so tiny that they can move right through a cell membrane and into the cell. (Remember diffusion? Here it is again.) One way cells can eat is to let tiny molecules of food and water *diffuse* through the membrane, just like perfume diffused through the wall of the balloon in the last chapter. This way, the cell can eat without having a mouth.

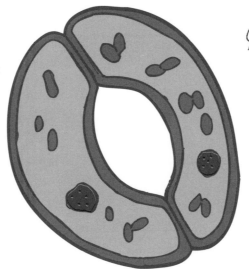

The cell membrane is fussy, though. It doesn't let every molecule through—just some of them, like molecules of food and water. When water diffuses through it's called by its own special name: **osmosis** (oz MO sis). Scientists call a membrane that only lets *some* things through a **semi-permeable** (sem eye PERM ee uh bull) membrane. That just means some things *can* go through, and some things *can't*.

I BET TONY'S CELLS ARE A LOT FUSSIER THAN HE IS!

Why do you think a cell would be so picky? In your science journal, imagine a cell that let *everything* in and out. What would happen? What would happen to a cell if it didn't let *anything* in or out?

LOSE SOMETHING?
Your body has trillions of cells, and is always working to make new ones to replace old ones. About 3 billion of your body's cells die every minute.

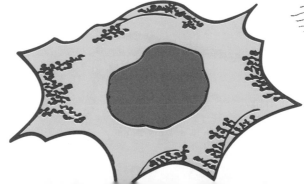

— SEE 'YA.. HAVE A GOOD NANO SECOND!

EXPERIMENT 1: COMING THROUGH!

You can create a model to show how cell membrane works.

WARNING IODINE IS POISONOUS! DO NOT DRINK IT!

Before you start: In this experiment, it's important to know what iodine does to cornstarch. Put a little cornstarch in a bowl. Add one drop of water. What happened? Add one drop of iodine. What happened? Make some notes in your journal. Now you're ready to start.

1. Put 1/3 cup of cornstarch into your plastic bag. Close the bag *tightly*. Wrap your rubber band *tightly* around the top to make sure no water can get in. This is your cell and cell membrane.

If any cornstarch got on the outside of the bag, rinse it all off before going to Step 2. Wash your hands, too, just in case.

2. Fill your bowl or jar halfway with water. Place your bag of cornstarch in the water. Make sure the part that has cornstarch in it is *under* the water. You can leave the top of the bag out of the water (to avoid any leaking.)

3. Add 20 drops of iodine to the water. Are there any changes in the cell? -in the water? Come back in 1/2 hour and check again. Has anything changed?

4. Take the bag out and open it.

Check for wetness inside. In your science journal, think out loud about these questions: Did water get in the cell? Did iodine get in? How do you know? Did cornstarch diffuse out of the cell and into the water? How do you know? Now sprinkle some cornstarch directly into the water in your bowl. What happens? Write down what the cell membrane kept in and what it kept out. Now write down what leaked out of the cell and what stayed in. Was there diffusion? osmosis? Is the bag semi-permeable?

INVESTIGATE SOME MORE!

Do the experiment again, but this time punch several small holes in your plastic bag. What happens? Is it still semi-permeable? Do you think a cell membrane is important? Why or why not?

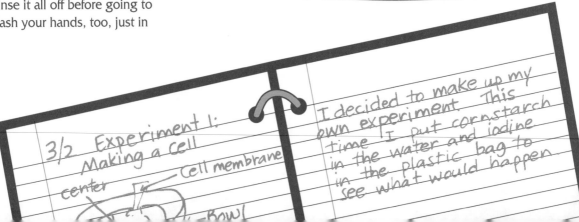

3/2 Experiment 1: Making a cell

center   Cell membrane

Bowl

I decided to make up my own experiment. This time I put cornstarch in the water and iodine in the plastic bag to see what would happen

EXPERIMENT 2: DIFFUSION CONFUSION

A plant's cells let food and water in by diffusion, too. Food and water in the soil diffuse into the plant's roots, and then diffuse into the plant's cells.

You've probably heard of acid rain. Acid rain changes what the plant diffuses in and out. In this experiment you'll be looking at how that can effect a growing plant.

1. Fill your cups almost to the top with soil. Plant one seed in each cup (follow directions on your seed packet to see how deep to plant them). With your marker, write TAP WATER on three of the cups, and ACID RAIN on the other three.

2. Fill one bottle with tap water. Test the water with your pH paper to find out the pH (anything below 7 is an acid). Stick a piece of masking tape on the bottle and write TAP WATER and the pH on it.

3. Fill your other bottle with water. Add a teaspoon of vinegar to the bottle, and test the pH. Keep adding vinegar until the pH is 4. With a pH of 4, this bottle will be similar to acid rain. Put tape on the bottle and write ACID RAIN, pH 4.

4. For the next few weeks, water the cups that say TAP WATER with your TAP WATER bottle, and the ACID RAIN cups with your ACID RAIN bottle. In your journal, draw pictures and write down what happens to the seeds. Which seeds grew the best? Which plants do you think were diffusing the food and water they needed? After a few weeks, cut open the plants and test the pH of the fluids inside each plant. What do you find?

SOUR NEWS

Pitlochry, Scotland, once had rainfall with pH of 2.4—that's as acid as lemon juice.

FIGHTING OAKS

Trees fight back if acid rain falls on their leaves. Their roots will absorb chemicals in the soil which change the pH back to the way they like it. Unfortunately, this only works if not too much acid rain falls.

INVESTIGATE SOME MORE!

Use your pH paper to test the soil in your community—at home, at the park, and at school. Make notes on what kind of things are growing, and how healthy the plants in each location appear to be. Which plants seem to do better in acid soil? Which do worse? Write down the results in your journal.

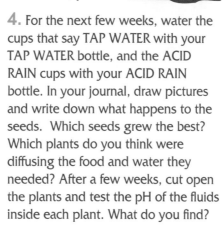

EXPLORE SOME MORE

A CELL O' JELLO

Remember reading that a cell was like a balloon full of jello? Well, it's time to build a giant-sized model of a cell, and you can use jello to do it. Not all cells look alike, but this experiment will show some things you'll find in an animal cell. The best part is you can eat it when you're done. The jello will make up the main body of the cell. Use pieces of fruit to show the different things that are inside the cell. The instructions and illustration below will show you how to put it all together and will describe some common things found in animal cells. Have an adult help you with the cooking. And remember: It's not dessert, it's science!

   jello mix—green or yellow is good
   an orange slice
   banana slices
   some pineapple chunks
   jello mold or bowl

WARNING HOT STOVES AND HOT JELLO CAN BE DANGEROUS! HAVE AN ADULT HELP WITH THE COOKING!

Cook the jello following the instructions on the package. The instructions will tell you when it's time to add your fruit slices. Use the illustrations below to help you make your cell.

Cytoplasm
(SIGH toe plaz um)
The main body of the cell
The jello is the cytoplasm

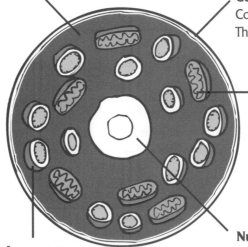

Cell membrane
Controls what goes in and out
The bowl will be your cell membrane

Mitochondria
(my toe KON dree ah)
Turns food into energy
Use six or seven pineapple chunks to show the mitochondria in your cell

Lysosomes
(LIE sih sohms)
Clean up all the junk in the cell
Use a dozen banana slices for the lysosomes

Nucleus
(NEW klee us)
Tells the cell what to do, and tells it how to make new cells
Use one orange slice for the nucleus

THE SAME ONLY DIFFERENT

A cell has everything it needs to eat, do work, get oxygen, and make more cells. So do we. But we don't look at all the same. You know a cell doesn't have a mouth, but it still can eat. It just has a different way of doing it. Look at the different parts of the cell. Now look at your own body. What things do you and a cell have in common? What things are different? How do you get the same job done?

FOR FURTHER EXPLORATION
Cells: Building Blocks of Life by Alvi Silverstein (Englewood Cliffs, NJ: 1969).
Food and Digestion by Steve Parker (New York: Franklin Watts, 1990).

TAKE A DEEP BREATH

Take a deep breath. Did you ever try to count how many times you inhale in a day? Too many to count! Why do we do all that breathing anyway? Why don't we breathe just once or twice a day?

Blame It on the Little Guys

Our body cells not only need food and water to do work, they also need oxygen. *Lots* of oxygen. We have millions of tiny cells asking for oxygen, so we have to breathe a lot.

When we breathe in, our lungs fill with air. Air has oxygen in it. (This oxygen has a special name when written down: O_2. That means it's really two oxygen molecules stuck together.) Right next to our lungs are thousands of little tiny blood vessels. Can you guess how the O_2 gets from our lungs to the nearby blood? Does it help to know that the lungs have a semi-permeable membrane? **(Hint:** Take a look at Chapters 5 and 6 again. If you were a molecule, how would *you* get places?)

Let's Trade

While the O_2 is moving from your lungs to your blood, your blood is giving something back—carbon dioxide (also called CO_2). This is waste from all the hard work your cells are doing.

Think of it as a swap: O_2 for CO_2. When you breathe out, you're breathing out carbon dioxide. That's why breathing *out* is just as important as breathing *in*. You want to get rid of all that CO_2. Your lungs have two important jobs: taking in oxygen and getting rid of carbon dioxide.

BREATHLESS
Some animals are extra good at holding their breath. Whales are mammals (not fish) and breathe air just like we do. However, a sperm whale can hold its breath for an hour and a half!

...AND THAT'S NO WHALE STORY!

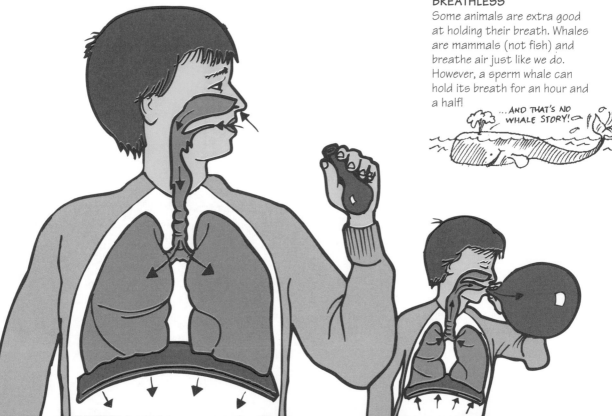

EXPERIMENT 1: HUFF AND PUFF

SUPPLIES
gallon jug
funnel (or the top part of
  a plastic bottle)
2-3 feet of rubber hose
sink or big plastic tub (a
  big dishpan is fine)
pen or marker

Do you always breathe the same way? Do your lungs always take in the same amount of oxygen each time? Use the experiment below to find out.

WARNING HAVE AN ADULT CUT THE BOTTLE AND PUT THE "X" IN THE FUNNEL.

1. If you're using a top of a plastic bottle instead of a funnel, cut off the top so you have a funnel shape. Cut an X in the side of the funnel, just big enough to let the hose push through. Not too big! Push one end of your hose through this X.

2. Place the funnel and hose into the sink with the small part pointing up. Make sure it lies flat on the bottom. Add water to cover the top of the funnel.

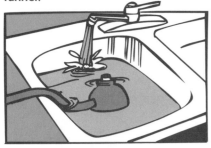

(Keep in mind: The sink has to be big enough to hold all this water *plus* another gallon.)

3. Fill the gallon jug with water. Put your fingers over the top, turn it over, and place the jug over the skinny end of the funnel.

Make sure no water runs out. **Note:** Make sure the place where the gallon jug and the funnel come together is UNDER WATER.

4. Now take a normal-sized breath and breathe into the hose. What happens? Use your marker to mark the water level on the jug.

5. Now take a *deep* breath and breathe into the hose. What happened this time? Make a mark on the side of the jar to show the water level.

BIG YAWN

Your body yawns when there's too much CO_2 in your lungs. A yawn makes you take a deep breath. When you exhale, you get rid of the extra CO_2. You yawn when you're tired because you're taking shallow breaths. For some reason (no one knows why) you also yawn if you see someone else yawn first. Try yawning in front of others and watch what happens!

HOW'S YOUR CO_2 LEVEL? I JUST WATCHED A RERUN OF "SPACE NERDS," SO MINE'S PRETTY LOW RIGHT NOW!

INVESTIGATE SOME MORE!

Have different people try this experiment. Make a mark on the side of the jar to show the water level each time. Have adults try it, too. Ask a friend who's an athlete or a singer to try it. Do you see any difference? What does this tell you about their lungs? Who else might fit into this category?

EXPERIMENT 2: AND IT COMES OUT HERE

SUPPLIES
large plastic bottle (a big soda bottle is good)
flexible drinking straw
rubber band
plastic bag
clay or wax
balloon
scissors
tape

Ever wonder how you push air in and out all day? This model of the lungs shows you how it works.

WARNING HAVE AN ADULT HELP YOU CUT OFF THE BOTTOM OF THE BOTTLE.

1. Have an adult help cut off the bottom of the bottle. Tape the plastic bag over the bottom, leaving some room so you can push and pull the plastic. Tape it securely around the outside of the bottle. Make sure you leave no gaps for air to go in or out.

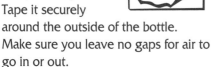

2. Slip one end of the straw into the balloon. Wrap the rubber band around tightly to keep it in place. This will be a lung. Lower the lung through the top of the bottle. Leave the top of the straw halfway out.

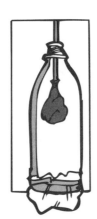

3. Use clay to hold the straw in place in the neck of the bottle, and to plug up the rest of the neck. Make sure there are no air holes or leaks in the clay. You need a tight seal for this to work.

CLAY

4. Pull out on the plastic bag on the bottom. What happens? Push in on the plastic bag. What happens now?

SWITCH-BREATHERS

Fish don't have lungs—they have gills which absorb oxygen from water. The exception is the lungfish. It not only has gills to get oxygen from the water, but it has lungs, too. If the pond suddenly dries up, they lay in the mud and use their lungs to breath until the pond fills up again.

O SOLE MIO

I DIDN'T KNOW YOU COULD SING!

SURE I CAN! WHY DO YOU THINK I HAVE LUNGS?

INVESTIGATE SOME MORE!

The muscle that pushes up and down in your body is the diaphragm (DI a fram). Place your fingers right below your ribs in the front. Take a deep breath. Can you feel it move? Keep your fingers there and sing a song. Why do you think singers have strong diaphragms?

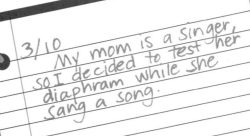

3/10 My mom is a singer, so I decided to test her diaphram while she sang a song.

EXPLORE SOME MORE

WHERE'S THE NOSE ON A ROSE?

Plants breathe, too, but not like us. Plants *take in* carbon dioxide, and *give out* oxygen. We return the favor by giving them carbon dioxide. What a team!

Plants don't exactly have noses, though. They have pores. Remember stomata? The stomata don't just let water evaporate, they let carbon dioxide in and oxygen out, too. (Since plants don't have lungs, can you guess how the molecules of oxygen and carbon dioxide move in and out?)

So where are these stomata? Use petroleum jelly to find out. Petroleum jelly will stop air from going through. It's like giving a plant a stuffy nose.

JUST THINKING ABOUT THIS EXPERIMENT LEAVES ME BREATHLESS!

For this experiment you'll need 3 small plants (of the same kind) and petroleum jelly.

1. Take your first plant and rub a coating of petroleum jelly all along the stem of the plant only. Don't get any on the leaves!

2. Take your second plant, and rub petroleum jelly all over the top side of the leaves only. Don't get any on the stem or the undersides of the leaves.

3. Take your third plant and rub petroleum jelly all over the underside of the leaves only.

4. Watch your three plants every day. Write down in your science journal what you see. Draw pictures of each plant. After a week, can you tell which plant has trouble breathing? How can you tell? Where are the stomata?

5. When you're done, clean off each plant with a solution of water with a little mild detergent so they can all breathe again.

FISH VERSUS FIDO

How fast you breathe is called your **respiratory rate.** To measure your respiratory rate, count how many times you inhale in a minute. Write it down in your science journal. This is your rate while resting. Now walk around the room or do jumping jacks. Take your rate again. This is your rate while active. Write it down.

YOU DO JUMPING JACKS... I'LL DO JUMPING JILLS!

But what about other people, and how about animals? Make a chart in your science journal and measure the respiratory rate of:

- an adult
- a baby
- an older person
- a large person
- an athlete

Go to a pet store and ask permission to watch and chart the respiratory rates for a:

- cat
- kitten
- dog
- fish
- lizard
- guinea pig
- any other interesting animals

Which rates are alike? Which are very different? Does age make a difference? What about size? What would you estimate the respiratory rate of an elephant might be?

I DON'T KNOW ABOUT HIS RESPIRATORY RATE BUT EVERY TIME HE HITS THE GROUND, I BET IT REGISTERS 3.2 ON THE RICHTER SCALE!!

Graph the results. The next time you go to a zoo, take your chart and write down rates for as many animals as you can. Are there any surprises? Was your guess about the elephant right?

FOR FURTHER EXPLORATION

The Lungs and Breathing by Brian R. Ward (New York: Franklin Watts, 1982).

O₂ TO GO

In the last chapter, your blood cells were sitting there near your lungs, picking up oxygen. Now they have to deliver it to your hungry cells. Your blood needs to travel to your toes and fingertips and everywhere else. But how is it going to get there?

We Deliver Anywhere

It all starts with your heart. Your heart is a pump. It *squeezes* together, pushing blood out and getting it moving. But your blood doesn't just slosh around inside you. It races through special tubes called **blood vessels.** Some of the vessels are really big (you can see some in your arms and legs, under the skin). As they get to your cells they get very tiny, so they can reach all your cells (the tiniest blood vessels are called **capillaries**).

That's why, no matter where you cut yourself, blood comes out. Blood has to be everywhere and reach all the cells in your body.

Do It Again

When your blood delivers oxygen, it also picks up the carbon dioxide the cells are getting rid of. All day long your blood goes back and forth between your cells and your lungs.

A FEW BILLBOARDS ALONG THIS CAPILLARY EXPRESSWAY WOULD CERTAINLY MAKE THE TRIP MORE INTERESTING!

(Can you guess why they call this your **circulatory system?**) It takes a lot of work to do this all day. That's why your heart is the strongest muscle in your body. It has to be! It never gets a day off, or even a nap. It pumps all day long, every day of your life.

Sometimes your body is working extra hard, so your cells need even *more* oxygen. What's a hard-working heart to do?

FAST DELIVERY!

Your blood makes a complete circuit around your body over 1,000 times a day. That's once every minute and a half. That's fast delivery!

SMELL AN APPLE A DAY!

You probably know that exercise and a good diet can keep your heart healthy. But did you know certain smells can, too? Scientists were surprised to find that when people smell spiced apples, their blood pressure goes down. It's still a mystery why this happens.

EXPERIMENT 1: FIND THE BEAT

SUPPLIES
1 1/2 feet of rubber
tubing
2 small funnels
scissors

How does your heart cope with hard work and hungry cells? Before you find out you have to be able to measure your heart beat. There are a few places where large blood vessels are close to the skin and you can feel your heart beating. This is called a **pulse.**

1. Use two fingers to feel for your pulse. The illustration shows two good places to look: the inside of your wrist (you've seen doctors hold wrists to check pulses), and in your neck.

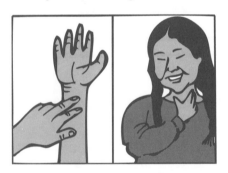

A lot of people think the pulse in the neck is easier to find, so try that one first.

2. Place your fingers flat against one of those spots until you feel a slight beating under your fingers. It's easier to find the pulse if your press down a little. You may have to feel around until you find the exact spot, so don't give up. Can you feel it? That's your blood being pushed through your blood vessels by your heart. Just to make sure you have it, ask a friend if you can check their pulse.

OR TRY THIS...

Doctors and nurses use a **stethoscope** to listen to your heart. You can make a home-made stethoscope that will help you hear your heart more clearly.

1. Find funnels whose small end will fit snugly into the ends of the rubber tubing. Put a funnel into each end of the tube.

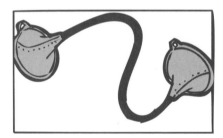

2. Find a quiet place. Hold one funnel against your heart, or the heart of a friend. Put the other funnel up against your ear. Listen carefully. What does it sound like? Why do you think the stethoscope helps you hear better?

UPSET? FIND FIDO!
Petting a cat or dog doesn't just feel good—it's good for you! Stroking your pet lowers your heart rate and blood pressure. Because of this, some hospitals and senior centers bring in dogs and cats for their patients to pet. Patients and pets both love it!

INVESTIGATE SOME MORE!
Wherever there's a large blood vessel near your skin, you can take a pulse. There are also strong pulses in your arms and legs. Can you find them?

EXPERIMENT 2: PUMP IT UP

SUPPLIES
paper to write on (your science journal will be great)
pen or pencil
a watch with a second hand
friends and family

Now that you can find your pulse, it's time to find out what your heart does to feed your hungry cells when your body is working extra hard.

1. Sit down and relax for a few minutes. Once you're relaxed, find your pulse or use your stethoscope to listen to your heart. Looking at the watch, count how many times your heart beats in a minute. This is called a **heart rate**. Write down the results in your journal.

2. Take a slow stroll around the block. Not too fast. As soon as you finish, count your heartbeats for one minute. Write it down.

3. Now do something active for 2 minutes. You can run around, do jumping jacks, or sit-ups—anything you want.

Find your pulse and count how many times your heart beats in a minute. Write it down. (By the way, are you sweating? How are your lungs doing?)

4. Ask an adult to take their resting heartbeat. Is it different from yours? Now ask other adults and friends. Write down the results. How do heartbeats change with age? size? Ask an athlete or two. How do their heartbeats compare? Once you've recorded a few people's heartbeats, can you come close to guessing what someone's heart rate will be? On what basis do you make your predictions?

'SCUSE ME, BUT WHEN YOU'VE RESTED FROM SCORING THIS TOUCHDOWN, CAN I RECORD YOUR HEARTBEAT?

A LONG STRANGE TRIP
If you laid all your blood vessels end to end, they'd wrap around the Earth almost 2-1/2 times.

THAT'S A TRIP I THINK I'LL PASS ON!

INVESTIGATE SOME MORE!
After you take a friend's heart rate for a minute, switch to counting their respiration rate for a minute. Write these numbers down side by side. When one changes, will the other change, too? Why or why not?

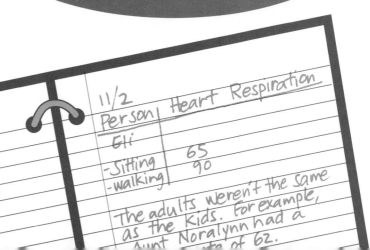

11/2
Person	Heart	Respiration
Eli		
-Sitting	65	
-Walking	90	

The adults weren't the same as the kids. For example, Aunt Noralynn had a [rate] of 62.

EXPLORE SOME MORE

ON THE LOOKOUT

Are there other rhythms in the body? Use your science journal to help you spot rhythms. Starting with when you wake up, and ending with when you get in bed, *every three hours* write down:

- Whether you feel tired or sleepy
- Whether you feel alert
- Whether you're hungry
- When you last ate a meal
- What your heart rate is
- What your respiration rate is
- What your body temperature is

(**Note:** Be very careful. You may want an adult take your temperature.)

If you're at school, explain to your teacher that you're doing an important science experiment. Maybe your experiment can be a class project!

You can learn a lot by doing this for one day, but patterns are easier to see if you do it for two or three days. Whatever you decide, don't forget to write down when you wake up and fall asleep.

Now for the fun of analyzing your data: What times of the day did you feel tired? alert? How did you feel before you ate? after you ate? Was your temperature the same all day? Were your heart and respiration rates high or low when you felt sleepy? Were they low or high when you felt alert?

Can you see any patterns? What does this tell you about your body? Write your ideas and discoveries in your science journal. What information was useful? Which information wasn't? What would you do differently next time?

Think of a way to share your data in the form of a picture or diagram.

FASCINATING RHYTHMS

The beating heart is probably the very first thing we hear. We hear our mother's heart before we're even born. For this experiment you'll need:
  stethoscope
  percussion instruments such as:
    drums
    sticks
    pots and pans
    logs or pieces of wood to hit with
     sticks
    cans or jars filled with sand or dry
     beans
    spoons to hit together
  friends

Maybe that's why people love rhythms so much. Make your own music by using your body's rhythms as a starting point.

Find or make percussion instruments. You can use the list above, or make your own. Gather a few friends together and make sure everyone has an instrument.

Start by listening to your heart, using your stethoscope. Beat on your drum to the same rhythm as your heart. Have a friend add the rhythm of their own breathing by beating on their instrument. One by one, have your friends join in, adding their own sound and rhythm.

You're making music from body rhythms! Add humming, singing, or chanting (more music made with your body) and let the rhythms move and change as they will. How does it sound? How does it feel?

FOR FURTHER EXPLORATION
The Heart and The Blood by Steve Parker (Franklin Watts, 1991).
How the Body Works by Ron Wilson (New York: Larousse, 1978).

BREAK IT DOWN

What did you have for lunch? Whatever it was, it was way too big for your blood to carry around. (Can you imagine your blood trying to move that tuna sandwich through your blood vessels?) All your food needs to be broken into tiny pieces first.

Take a Big Bite

That's why teeth are so important. They don't just look great when you smile—they have a job to do. Your teeth rip and chew your food into smaller pieces. If you look at your teeth in the mirror, you can see they're not all shaped alike. The ones in the front are good at taking bites out of things. The sharp ones (they look like dog teeth) are good at ripping meat. The flat ones in the back are good at grinding things like vegetables. They chew up the food so it's small enough to go to your stomach.

Fabulous Spit

Nobody seems to say anything nice about spit. (If you want to get fancy, call it **saliva** [sal EYE v].) But spit has an important job to do. It starts breaking down your food right in your mouth, even before it gets to your stomach. It contains a special chemical that breaks down the molecules in some foods. It also makes food nice and wet, so it's easier to swallow. Did you ever try to swallow something really dry? It's hard! So try to think nice thoughts about spit.

Once your teeth and saliva have done their job, your food is still too big. That's why your stomach makes juices that break down your food into even smaller pieces. (These juices taste really bad. If you've ever gotten sick and vomited, you've tasted food mixed with these juices. Yuck!)

Once your stomach is done, it opens up a hole in the bottom. This leads to the small intestine, a tube that has even *more* juices to break down your food. By now your food is just the right size for your cells to eat. Can you guess who will deliver it to them? How do you think it will get from inside the intestines all the way to the cells? Draw a picture in your journal of the route you think it will take.

OPEN WIDE
Animals with lots of sharp teeth eat mostly meat. Animals with mostly flat teeth eat only grass or plants. This is how scientists can look at a dinosaur skeleton and guess whether it was a ferocious meat-eater or a gentle grazer. They check out the teeth!

AN IDEA TO CHEW ON
Just by looking at an animal's teeth, you can tell a lot about what it eats.

JUDGING BY THESE ROTTEN TEETH, I'D SAY WE'VE GOT OURSELVES A RARE CANDY-EATING LOLLIPOSAURUS!!

EXPERIMENT 1: THE DAILY GRIND

It's hard to get a good look at all your teeth in the mirror. And mirrors don't give you a good view of your teeth doing their job—grinding. Now you can make a mold of your teeth and see them in action.

WARNING ! YOU'LL BE PUTTING THE CLAY IN YOUR MOUTH, SO MAKE SURE YOU ONLY BUY CLAY THAT SAYS "NONTOXIC" ON THE PACKAGE!

1. Shape your clay into two wedges the size of your mouth.

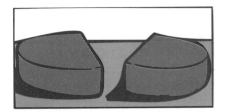

Make sure the wedges are thick enough so you can bite into them but not *through* them. Don't make it too big or it won't fit in your mouth. Now put one in your mouth and press your top teeth into the wedge. Make sure your get all your teeth. Now take it out carefully. Do the same thing with the other wedge, this time making an impression of your bottom teeth. Now brush your teeth to get all the clay off! (Don't forget to spit!)

2. You should be able to see imprints of all your teeth in the clay wedges. Now put them on a table. Cut your stiff paper into a long strip, 2 inches wide. Wrap this all around the top edge of your wedges and tape them.

This strip will hold in the plaster of paris, so make sure it's tight against the sides.

3. Put a cup of plaster of paris in your mixing bowl. Slowly mix in water, a little at a time, until you can just pour it. Keep it thick. Pour this into your molds and jiggle them so plaster sinks into all the places your teeth were. Wait overnight for the plaster to harden.

4. Remove the tape and paper. Slowly and carefully peel off the clay. Make sure you don't accidentally break any of the plaster mold! Now you have a mold of your teeth. Put the tops and bottoms together. Can you see how they fit? How many different kinds of teeth can you spot? Try to guess what each kind of tooth does.

MORE MOUTHWASH, PLEASE

The toothbrush was first invented in China over 500 years ago. Back then they didn't have nylon to make the bristles, so they had to use something else—animal hair!

HEY...GO FIND YOURSELF ANOTHER TOOTHBRUSH!

INVESTIGATE SOME MORE!

Ask an adult to let you make a mold of their teeth. (Ask really nicely.) How are they different from yours? How many are there? Are they the same size and shape? Do teeth change over time? Can you guess how old someone is by their teeth?

EXPERIMENT 2: THE GREAT SPIT EXPERIMENT

SUPPLIES
3 small bowls
iodine
cornstarch
water
tablespoon
measuring cup
mixing spoon
saliva

Time to take a look at your hardworking spit. What's it doing while you're eating dinner?

WARNING IODINE IS POISONOUS! DO NOT DRINK IT!

1. In the measuring cup, mix together a cup of water and a tablespoon of cornstarch.

Put some of this mixture into each of the three bowls.

2. Put a drop of iodine into one of the bowls.

Iodine turns black when it touches starch. (Remember the experiment in Chapter 2?) Does the mixture in the bowl turn black? Is this a starch or not?

3. Put a tablespoon of spit into the second bowl, and mix it around. (It's messy, but remember, you're spitting for science!)

Wait two minutes. Now add a drop of iodine. What happens?

4. Put a tablespoon of spit into the third bowl and mix it. Wait five minutes. Add a drop of iodine. What happens? Is this a starch? What is the job of saliva?

MIND OVER MATTER

A Russian named Pavlov rang a bell whenever he fed his dogs. After a while, as soon as he rang the bell his dogs would start to salivate whether they smelled food or not—their brains were sure food was coming! Your body does the same thing. If you even think about food, your body will start making more saliva, just in case.

INVESTIGATE SOME MORE!

To see what saliva does to fats, add saliva to two tablespoons of oil. Mix it together, then do the test for fats as follows: **The Fat Test:** Rub the stuff you're testing on a piece of a brown paper bag. If it turns the bag **translucent** (which means some light shows through), then there's fat present. Does saliva change fats?

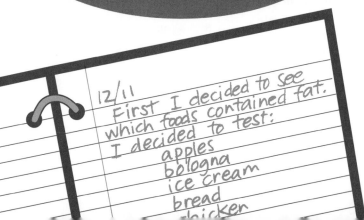

12/11
First I decided to see which foods contained fat. I decided to test:
apples
bologna
ice cream
bread
chicken

EXPLORE SOME MORE

MONSTER MOUTH

When monster movies and comic books want to make a creature look scary, they often give it huge teeth. Sometimes the actor playing the monster can hardly close his mouth because his teeth are so big. How's a creature supposed to eat with teeth like that?

HAVE YOU EVER TRIED EATING MASHED POTATOES THROUGH A STRAW..?!

It's your turn to make teeth for a monster. Make the teeth as scary as you want, but make sure they can still do their job—mash food into pieces. You'll need non-toxic clay (get the kind that dries by itself), fine sandpaper, and toothpicks.

1. Decide what your monster eats—broccoli? -meat? -rocks? (Remember, it's *your* monster; you can make it eat anything you want.) Draw a picture of it in your science journal.

2. Now decide what kind of teeth it will need to eat that stuff—sharp teeth? flat teeth? teeth shaped like files? Should it have just one kind of tooth or many kinds? Then decide *how many* teeth it has. Keep in mind: The top and bottom teeth have to fit together when your monster closes its mouth.

3. Now it's time to start building. Start by cutting two flat wedges of clay to build your teeth on.

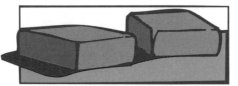

One will be the top set of teeth and the other will be the bottom. Start shaping your teeth, one by one, and putting them in place on the wedge. You might have to use toothpicks to hold them in place if they're really big. (Clay sometimes falls over.)

4. Wait for your masterpiece to dry. When it's done, put the two sets of teeth together. Do they fit? Will your monster be eating its own gums? Will they work as teeth? Use sandpaper to sand down any teeth that need to be changed.

Show your teeth to some friends. What do they think your monster eats? You might even want to use clay to build a whole monster head. Leave room to put in those teeth!

TOOTHLESS

Some critters don't have any teeth at all, but they can still eat. Here's a list of some beings that eat without teeth. In your science journal, make guesses (some are easier than others) about what they eat and how they eat it. Use an encyclopedia for help. Would teeth help or hurt each animal? Would they starve if they had teeth? Try to think of other examples of living things that don't have teeth. Are teeth always a good idea?

Hummingbirds	Catfish
Blue whales	Jellyfish
Earthworms	Starfish
Ants	Clams
Sea anemones	Bluejays
Jellyfish	Slugs
Spiders	Woodpeckers
Frogs	Ducks
Squids	

DID YOU KNOW?

The average person eats about 1,000 pounds of food a year. That's a lot of chewing!

WHEN MY DOG EATS, IT'S MORE LIKE INHALING THAN CHEWING!

FOR FURTHER EXPLORATION

The Body Atlas by Steve Parker (London: Dorling Kindersley, 1993).
You Can't Sneeze with Your Eyes Open and Other Freaky Facts about the Human Body by Barbara Seuling (New York: Dutton, 1986).

WHO GETS THE LEFTOVERS?

You know what happens once food gets in your mouth. But what about the food that you don't eat? Think of all the stuff you leave on your plate—the half-eaten sandwich, the pile of soggy spinach, the lima beans. What happens to it all? Is there a mountain of uneaten lima beans somewhere on the planet? If you're not eating them, who is?

HERE'S MY THEORY: ALL UNEATEN BEANS IN THE WORLD ARE SHIPPED TO SOUTH AMERICA WHERE THEY FORM THE MOUNTAINS IN PERU WHICH ACCOUNTS FOR THE NAME OF ITS CAPITAL CITY LIMA!!

More for Us

Lucky for us, the world is full of very hungry bacteria and molds who just love lima beans and half-eaten sandwiches. And everything else you don't eat. Bacteria are really, really small—their whole body is only one cell big! But there are lots of them. When you throw out your food, bacteria will break it down into tiny pieces, just like your stomach does.

That's why there aren't any mountains of uneaten lima beans (thank goodness). The bacteria and molds ate them.

Helpful Worms

Bacteria aren't the only ones who help break down garbage. There's another garbage-eater around who's actually big enough to watch in action—the earthworm. People who know a lot about earthworms, like gardeners and farmers, think earthworms are wonderful! In the next two experiments you'll watch both bacteria and earthworms do their job. Maybe you'll start to think they're pretty wonderful, too.

DID YOU KNOW?

Earthworms don't use lungs to breathe—they use slime! The slime on their skin picks up oxygen. Their skin is a semi-permeable membrane, so oxygen diffuses right through their skin into their blood vessels. A dry, unslimy earthworm couldn't breathe!

For experiments with molds see *The Inside Story!*, Chapter 5. You can also investigate recycling in *Power Up!*, Chapter 10.

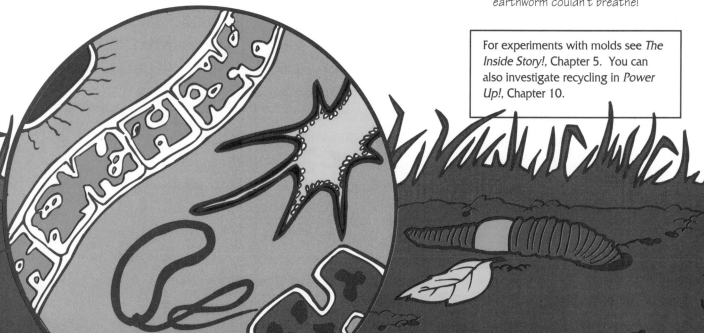

EXPERIMENT 1: BACTERIA ATE MY BREAKFAST

There are some things even bacteria won't eat. Maybe you've heard someone say "This isn't **biodegradable.**" That means no matter how long it stays in a pile of garbage, it will never get eaten. In this experiment, see if you can find which things are biodegradable and which aren't.

1. Fill your containers about half full with soil.

2. Cut the apple, bread, plastic wrap, paper, foil, and vegetable so they're about the same size as the cornflake.

3. Place each piece in its own container. Put them right on top of the soil.

4. Cover with a sprinkling of soil. Sprinkle some water on the soil (not too wet, just moist!).

5. Check every few days to see what's happening. Brush aside the soil and take a look. Cover up your pieces again when you're done.

In your science journal, keep track of how everything looks. What's breaking down? What looks exactly the same? Which things do you think are biodegradable? Why do you think some things break down, and others don't?

SOMETIMES WHEN I WISE-OFF, I'M TOLD I'LL END UP EATING MY OWN WORDS... I WONDER IF MY WORDS ARE BIODEGRADABLE?

INVESTIGATE SOME MORE!

Where does the garbage in your town go? Find out by calling the company or government agency who picks up your garbage. What do they do with it once they take it? Ask an adult to take you to see where it gets dumped. Do you think it's important that garbage be biodegradable?

3/1

Day 1

Apple - no change
Carrot - no change
Bread - no change
          no change

Day 2

Apple - turned a little brown
Carrot - looks the same
Bread - I think this is starting to change. It's pretty dirty.

EXPERIMENT 2: QUIET! WORMS AT WORK

How do worms eat garbage? Create your own worm farm and find out.

1. Layer your jar with the different kinds of soil.

Stop when you're 2 inches from the top. Add water to make the soil moist throughout the jar. (Not too much! Worms can drown! That's why they come up onto the sidewalk when it rains a lot. But make it moist enough so they can stay slimy and breathe.)

2. Now sprinkle the leaves over the soil, and add your worms.

3. Once the worms are nice and cozy in the earth, put the apple peelings on top of the soil.

4. Place the jar in a cool, dark place (a closet is good). They like the dark.

Check the jar every day to see what's happening. In your science journal write down what the worms are doing. Does the soil look different? What is happening to the leaves? What about the apple? Why do you think worms are great to have around?

Keep your worms happy. Let them go when the experiment is over.

SUPPLIES

a large jar
soil (two or three different kinds if you can find them)
worms
dead leaves you find on the ground
apple
water

THE SIDEWALK'S ALL YOURS!
There are all kinds of earthworms. In South Africa, there are earthworms that get VERY big—22 feet long to be exact.

INVESTIGATE SOME MORE!

Fix another jar exactly the same way as your earthworm farm, but don't add any worms. Dump the dirt from your first worm farm onto a newspaper. Then dump the soil from the worm farm-without worms onto a separate newspaper. Compare the two soils. Look at them with your loupe and do some drawings. Do you see any differences?

EXPLORE SOME MORE

IT'S NOT GARBAGE, IT'S ART!

Artists use all kinds of materials in their art: paints, metal, old machinery, newspapers, pieces of wood—anything that strikes their fancy. They even use garbage!

Start your art by collecting stuff that gets thrown away. (Remember to ask permission before you take anything.) Old toys, parts of furniture, old rugs, torn books, string, wire, old pictures, empty cereal boxes, plastic bottles, wheels from toys. Collect as many different kinds of junk as you can. Make sure everything is clean, and don't use anything that has sharp edges that can hurt you. When assembling your pile of junk, make sure you get things that have different shapes and textures: you probably don't want all your junk to look alike. (But maybe you do. And the artist is never wrong.)

Once you have a nice big pile, it's time to assemble it into your art. You might want to use:

tape (all kinds)	glue
paint	markers
string	construction paper
anything else you can think of!	

Now it's time to create your masterpiece. Just looking at your pile should give you ideas about what you want to make. When you're done, name your art and find a place to display it. Does it still look like junk to you?

DELICIOUS DIRT

The best way to make dirt delicious is to add compost. Compost is what's left over when you let hungry bacteria feast on your leftovers. It looks like rich, dark soil, and plants love it.

The most important thing you need to make compost is a place to put it. This place will be called your compost pile. If you have a backyard, you can make one there. If you don't, ask about starting a compost pile at school.

Make a circle of chicken wire. This will hold the pile together while still letting it get plenty of air (air is important for composting).

Put straw or branches on the bottom of the pile (this helps air get in the pile, too). Create the pile in layers, starting with straw, then a layer of kitchen scraps or grass clippings and then a layer of dirt. Then start over again.

Here are items that can go in the "kitchen scraps" layer:
- any vegetables
- any fruits, fruit skins, or rinds
- old bread
- coffee grounds
- eggshells
- grass clippings
- any beans and legumes
- grains

Things that should *never* go in a compost pile include:
- meat (it attracts flies and rodents)
- cheese
- oils or butter
- milk or dairy products

Always keep your pile moist but not wet. The bacteria will start eating your kitchen scraps right away. All their activity makes the inside of the pile warm—in cold weather, in fact, you can even see your compost pile steam! Make compost more quickly by turning your pile over every few weeks. In anywhere from three to six months your pile of garbage will turn into a pile of rich, dark compost. Plants everywhere will thank you for it.

DID YOU KNOW?
People throw away lots of things that could be turned into compost. In most cases, 18% to 30% of the garbage people throw away could have been used in a compost pile.

IT'S NICE TO KNOW THAT AFTER FILLING SOME KID'S STOMACH, YOU CAN STILL KEEP ON GIVING!

FOR FURTHER EXPLORATION
Worms Eat My Garbage by Mary Appelhof (Kalamazoo, MI: Flower Press, 1982).
Cartons, Cans and Orange Peels: Where Does Your Garbage Go? by Joanne Foster (New York: Houghton Mifflin, 1991).

acid rain rain that has a low, acidic pH, usually because of pollution

adaptation the process whereby an organism modifies itself in order to survive better within the conditions of its environment

arboretums a place for studying and viewing trees and plants

adobe sun-dried bricks made of clay and straw

air pressure the force of air pushing on things

bacteria tiny organisms that are only one cell big

barometer a tool for measuring air pressure

biodegradable anything that can be broken down by natural forces

blood vessels tubes which carry blood throughout the body

botanical garden a garden for studying and viewing plants

capillaries the tiniest blood vessels that bring blood to and from the cells

carbon dioxide one carbon atom and two oxygen atoms (CO_2); humans and animals exhale CO_2 when they breathe

cell membrane the structure around a cell that holds the cell together and lets food and wastes in and out of the cell

circulatory system the parts of the body that pump and deliver blood, including the heart, blood vessels, and capillaries

cirrus clouds thin, wispy clouds

condensation a reduction to a denser form, as from steam to water

cumulonimbus clouds the tallest clouds, growing high into the air

cumulus clouds white fluffy clouds that usually mean nice weather

cytoplasm the jellylike substance of a cell, outside the nucleus and inside the cell membrane

diffusion the spreading out of molecules to other places

digestion eating and breaking down food until it can be used by the body's cells

evaporation conversion of a liquid into a vapor or gas

heart rate how often a heart beats

lysosomes the part of the cell that cleans up the cytoplasm

mitochondria the part of a cell that turns food into energy

nucleus the part of the cell that carries instructions on how the cell should act and how the cell can make new cells

osmosis occurs when water molecules move from one place to another, especially across a membrane

pores tiny holes in the skin that allow sweat to move to the surface of the skin

potpourri a mix of dried flowers, spices, and herbs, often kept in a jar and used for scent

pulse the throbbing of blood vessels as the heart pumps blood through them

respiratory rate how often a person inhales and exhales

saliva the watery substance in the mouth that moistens and breaks down food; spit

semi-permeable membrane a cell membrane that lets only certain things move through it

stethoscope a device that makes it easier to hear the heart beating

stomata the holes in a leaf that let oxygen, carbon dioxide, and water diffuse through

stratus clouds dark clouds that form a low blanket over the sky

transpiration the movement of gases and water vapor out of a plant through the stomata

water cycle the process where rain falls, evaporates, condenses, and falls as rain again

water vapor water in the air, especially when diffused as in the atmosphere